A FROGGY FABLE

JOHN LECHNER

CANDLEWICK PRESS

CAMBRIDGE, MASSACHUSETTS

![Knowsley Council]

Knowsley Library Service

Please return this book on or
before the date shown below

2 7 MAR 2024

You may return this book to any Knowsley Library
For renewal please telephone:

0151 443 3734
School Library Service 0151 443 4285

Visit us at: **yourlibrary.knowsley.gov.uk**

f @knowsleylibraries   @knowsleylibraryreal   @knowsleylib

For my mother and father

First edition 2005

Library of Congress Cataloging-in-Publication Data is available.

Library of Congress Catalog Card Number 2004051880

ISBN 0-7636-2123-4

2 4 6 8 10 9 7 5 3 1

Printed in Singapore

This book was typeset in Clichee.
The illustrations were done in watercolor and ink.

Candlewick Press
2067 Massachusetts Avenue
Cambridge, Massachusetts 02140

visit us at www.candlewick.com

Once there was a frog who lived under a rock by himself.

Every day he did the same thing.
He swam into the pond to eat breakfast.

He jumped onto a log to enjoy the sun.

Then he swam back to his hole under the big rock.
It was a simple life, but he liked it because it was
always the same.

Then one day, things started to change. . . .

A family of otters moved into the pond and started splashing around.

"Hey," said the frog, "I don't like those otters splashing in my pond."

A flock of blue jays moved into the trees overhead, and they squawked ALL the time.

"Hey, I don't like those birds making noise," the frog said.

And one day, lightning struck the tallest pine tree, which crashed into the water, spilling pine needles everywhere.

"Hey, I don't like that tree in my pond!" said the frog.

But there was nothing he could do about it.

The frog crawled into the back of his hole and stayed there.

He heard a voice behind him.
"Why are you so sad?" It was a small caterpillar.

"I'm sad because everything is changing," said the frog.

"I'm glad things change," the caterpillar replied.
"Someday I hope to change into a butterfly.
Trees change . . . flowers change . . . even
mountains and mighty rivers."

The frog just turned back toward the wall—he wanted to cry.

The caterpillar left, but the frog stayed in his hole.

Then one morning, something utterly unexpected happened. . . .

The rock over the frog's hole was lifted into the air.

To the poor frog's bewilderment, a jar came down on top of him . . .

and he was whisked away in the hands of a young boy.

Needless to say, nothing like this had ever happened to the frog before.

The terrified frog was jostled and bumped on the boy's bike.
They traveled for a long time, when suddenly the bike hit a rock. . . .

The jar went flying,

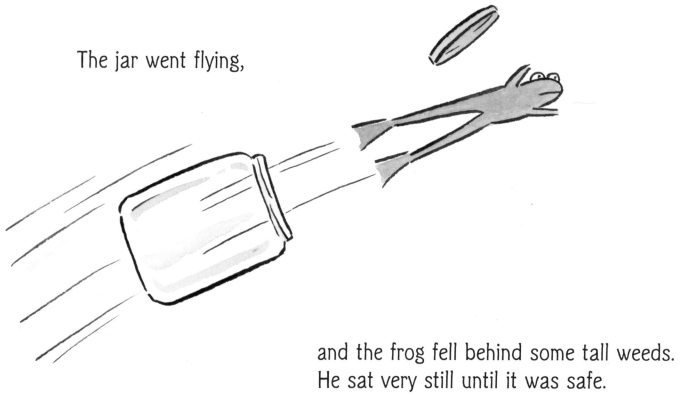

and the frog fell behind some tall weeds.
He sat very still until it was safe.

When the frog finally crept out, he found himself in a strange and unfamiliar place. He was lost.

The frog wandered until it got dark, then took shelter for the night in a hollow tree.

The next morning he kept on hopping, but just seemed to get more lost. Weeks went by, and the frog encountered many dangers . . .

and many wonders.

Squawk! Squawk!

Then one afternoon, when he had just about given up all hope of finding his home, he heard a noise from far away—a familiar noise.

He raced through the forest toward the sound.
As he got closer, he heard splashing.

Finally, he emerged into a clearing . . .

and saw a beautiful pond. HIS pond.

He was so happy to see the blue jays flapping overhead.
He was so happy to see the otters splashing in the water.

He was even happy to see the fallen tree, right where he'd
left it—he knew he was home.

True, his old rock had been torn away, but he found a perfect spot to dig another hole, with an even better view.

After that day, the frog didn't mind so much when things changed—he could handle anything.

He even tried something new once in a while.

And things were never the same again.